Letting Swift River Go

Jane Yolen

Illustrated by

Barbara Cooney

Little, Brown and Company
Boston Toronto London

For Janet Grenzke, who knows the Quabbin well —J.Y.

For the people of the Swift River Valley —B.C.

The Quabbin Valley Association of
Historical Societies provided background for this book.

Text copyright © 1992 by Jane Yolen
Illustrations copyright © 1992 by Barbara Cooney

First Edition

Library of Congress Cataloging-in-Publication Data

Yolen, Jane.
   Letting Swift River go / Jane Yolen; illustrated by Barbara
Cooney. —1st ed.
   p. cm.
Summary: Relates Sally Jane's experience of changing times
in rural America, as she lives through the drowning of the Swift River
towns in western Massachusetts to form the Quabbin Reservoir.
ISBN 0-316-96899-4
[1. Swift River (Mass.)—Fiction. 2. Massachusetts—Fiction.
3. Country life—Fiction. 4. Change—Fiction.] I. Cooney,
Barbara, 1917– ill. II. Title.
PZ7.Y8Le   1992
[E]—dc20   90-47909

10 9 8 7 6 5 4 3 2 1

NIL

Published simultaneously in Canada by Little, Brown & Company (Canada) Limited

Printed in Italy

The illustrations were painted in watercolor on D'Arches watercolor paper with the
addition of Prismacolor pencil and some pastel.

Author's Note

The Quabbin Reservoir is near my house,
one of the largest bodies of fresh water in New England.
It is a lovely wilderness;
eagles soar overhead and deer mark out their paths.
But once it was a low-lying valley called Swift River,
surrounded by rugged hills.
There were towns in the valley filled with hardworking folks
whose parents and grandparents had lived there all their lives.
Then, between 1927 and 1946, all the houses
and churches and schools—the markers of their lives—
were gone forever under the rising waters.

The drowning of the Swift River towns
to create the Quabbin was not a unique event.
The same story—only with different names—
has occurred all over the world
wherever nearby large cities have had powerful thirsts.
Such reservoirs are trade-offs, which, like all trades,
are never easy, never perfectly fair.

Wh+en I was six years old
the world seemed a very safe place.
The wind whispered comfortably
through the long branches
of the willow by my bedroom window.
Mama let me walk to school all alone
along the winding blacktop,
past the Old Stone Mill,
past the Grange Hall,
past our church,
not even meeting up with
Georgie Warren or Nancy Vaughan
till the crossroads.

Georgie and I fished the Swift River
in the bright days of summer,
catching brown trout out of the pools
with a pin hook and a bit of thread.
We played mumblety-peg
in the graveyard
and picnicked on Grandpa Will's stone,
the black one that stayed warm all day
by soaking up the hot summer sun.

And many a summer night
I slept out under the backyard maples
with Nancy Vaughan.
We'd listen to the trains
starting and stopping along Rabbit Run,
their long whistles lowing into the dark,
startling the screech owl
off its perch on the great elm.
Lying there, looking up
at the lengthening shadows of trees,
we'd see the fireflies
winking on and off and on.

One night Nancy Vaughan
and her cousin Sara from the city
brought three mason jars to my house.
We caught fireflies in them,
holding our hands over the open tops.
Mama came out to watch.
She shook her head.
"You have to let them go, Sally Jane,"
she said to me.
So I did.

In the deep winter
Papa harvested ice
from Greenwich Lake,
and Mama kept the stove going
in the house all day and all night.
I slept under three eiderdowns
and Grandma's quilt.
Later, in March,
we put buckets up on all the maples,
dipping our fingers down into the sap
and tasting the thin sweetness.

But then everything began to change.
The men went to the Grange Hall
time after time after time. The women, too.
Only nobody asked us kids.
They all listened to men from Boston
because the city of Boston, sixty miles away,
needed lots of water.
Boston had what Papa called
"a mighty long thirst,"
and no water to quench it.
We had water here in the valley:
good water, clear water,
clean water, cold water,
running between the low hills.
We could trade water for money,
or water for new houses,
or water for a better life.
So it was voted in Boston to drown our towns
that the people in the city might drink.

First we moved the graves:
Grandpa Will's black stone,
and the Doubledays and the Downings,
the Metcalfs and the Halls.
Papa read the headstones on the trucks
as he helped gather the small remains,
hauling them to the new cemetery
where everything would be fresh and green.
Sometimes all the men
found were buttons or teeth
or a few thin bones.
Papa said they left the Indians
where they lay.
No one wanted to bother with them,
but I thought it right
they remain in sacred ground.
The blackflies were fierce,
Papa said, fierce.
He had bites under his eyes,
swollen like tears.

Then the governor sent his "woodpeckers"
to clear the scrub and brush,
to cut down all the trees:
the maples and elms,
the willows and sycamores,
and the great spreading oaks.
They were stacked like drinking straws
along the roads,
then hauled away.

Our houses came next.
Some were bulldozed.
One great push and they went over
after one and two centuries
of standing strong
against wind and snow and rain.
Georgie and I watched them push down
the Old Stone Mill
till the windows of one wall
stared out like empty eyes
at the far-off hills.

Mr. Baxter's house went by truck
along the blacktop
to its new home in another town,
slow as any child going to school.
Nancy and I ran alongside for a ways,
but it had more breath than we did.
We stopped, panting,
and watched till it was out of sight.
Then Mama and Papa and I
moved away to New Salem,
one big hill over, and into a tiny house
where my room was warm all winter long.
Nancy and her folks went to the city
to be near her cousin Sara.
I never heard where Georgie went,
never even got to say good-bye.

Strangers came with their big machines,
building tunnels and caissons,
the Winsor Dam and the Goodnough Dike.
Papa brought me over to watch
most Friday afternoons.
"You've got to remember, Sally Jane," he said.
"Remember our town."
But it didn't *seem* like our town anymore.
There were no trees, no bushes,
no gardens, no fences,
no houses, no churches, no barns, no halls.
Just a long, gray wilderness,
just a hole between the hills.

The waters from the dammed rivers
moved in slowly and silently.
They rose like unfriendly neighbors
halfway up the sides of the hills,

covering Dana and Enfield,
Prescott and Greenwich,
all the little Swift River towns.
It took seven long years.

Much later, when I was grown,
Papa and I rowed out on the Quabbin Reservoir.
Behind us we left a bubble trail.
Through the late afternoon
and well into the evening
we sat in the little boat
and Papa pointed over the side.
"Look, Sally Jane," he said,
"that's where the road to Prescott ran,
there's the road to Beaver Brook,
that's the spot the church stood
where we had you baptized.
And the school.
And the Grange Hall.
And the Old Stone Mill.
We won't be seeing those again."
I looked.
I thought I could see the faint outlines,
but I could not read the past.
Little perch now owned those streets,
and bass swam over the country roads.
A rainbow trout leaped after a fly,
and the water rings rippled through
my father's careful mapping.

When it got dark
the stars came out,
reflecting in the water,
winking on and off and on like fireflies.
I leaned over the side of the boat
and caught the starry water
in my cupped hands.
For a moment I remembered
the wind through the willow,
the trains whistling on Rabbit Run,
the crossroads where I had met
Georgie Warren and Nancy Vaughan.
Gone, all gone, under the waters.

Then I heard my mother's voice
coming to me over the drowned years.
"You have to let them go, Sally Jane."
I looked down into the darkening deep,
smiled,

      and did.